ST. JOHN'S LUTHERAN
ELEMENTARY SCHOOL
For a Christ-Centered Education
3521 Linda Vista Ave.
Napa, California

ST. JOHN'S LUTHERAN
ELEMENTARY SCHOOL
For a Christ-Centered Education
3521 Linda Vista Ave.
Napa, California

MORE AESOP'S FABLES

PUBLISHED BY PETER HADDOCK LIMITED,
BRIDLINGTON, ENGLAND
PRINTED IN ITALY

ISBN 07105 0247 8

The Wolf and the Lamb

A long time ago, a big, bad wolf roamed in the forests in search of food. The forests in those days were very large and full of all sorts of small animals. The wolf usually had no trouble finding himself a meal in such surroundings.

One day, the big, bad wolf came across a little white lamb playing in the meadow. The wolf was very hungry and had visions of how he could eat the lamb and how tasty it would be. His only problem was that he did not want people to see him as a big, bad wolf, which he in fact was. So, he sat and thought of a good excuse which would be acceptable to all the people. He must find a reason to slaughter the little lamb to enable him to satiate his growing hunger.

At first, the wolf could not think of any reason for killing the lamb. After all, there was plenty of food in the forest. However, as he watched the lamb he did not see it drinking from the pool, instead he only had visions of the wonderful meal the lamb would make.

The wolf crept closer to the pool until he was standing above the lamb. However, he did not immediately pounce on the lamb but stood watching, while he finally decided what to do. Eventually, the lamb saw the wolf and began to shake. He was so frightened.

The wolf, who had now decided what to do, called to the lamb in a friendly voice. He asked the lamb to join him on the ledge. The lamb was very frightened but was too small to run away and he could not see his mother anywhere. So he climbed onto the ledge where he expected to meet his fate.

The wolf did not pounce upon him as he had expected, but instead began to speak. "Last year you called me many terrible names, names which I did not like and which upset me very much," said the wolf.

The lamb was amazed and in a shaky voice replied, "I am just a baby and was only born this year, therefore, as I was not even here last year it could not have been me. You appear to have mistaken me for another lamb, so if you do not mind I shall go on my way."

"No!" bellowed the wolf, "I am not mistaken, I am never wrong, and I do know you. You are the one who ate my dinner."
"But I did not eat your dinner as I am unable to eat and can only drink," said the lamb quivering.
"Then it must have been you who drank all my water — now I remember."
"But I cannot drink water, I can only drink the milk of my mother as I am still very young."

"But I can eat and I can drink," said the wolf, "as I am very big."

The lamb began to shake more furiously.

"And as I am very big and also very hungry I am going to eat you for my dinner," growled the wolf. With this the wolf jumped on the lamb and devoured him. Then the wolf having satisfied his hunger fell asleep without any feelings of remorse.

The moral of the story being. "People who want to do something bad can always find an excuse ."

The Ant and the Grasshopper

One hot summer's day, a grasshopper was sitting under the shade of a tree watching some ants who, in spite of the heat, were carrying enormous loads of food to their nest. These loads were to be their supplies for the long winter months.

The loads were very large and heavy and occasionally the ants stopped to rest. All the time, the grasshopper sat in the shade of the tree watching the ants work and singing tunes to himself. He thought the ants were rather stupid working so hard.

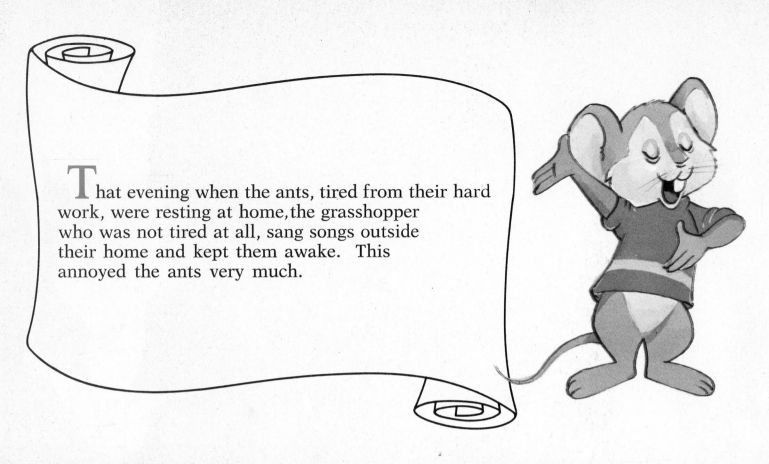

That evening when the ants, tired from their hard work, were resting at home, the grasshopper who was not tired at all, sang songs outside their home and kept them awake. This annoyed the ants very much.

After a few weeks had passed, the grasshopper noticed the weather was not so hot and all the leaves turned yellow and began to fall to the ground. The ants carried more and more food to their nest.

S oon the grasshopper realised what was happening. Winter was approaching. The ants disappeared and snow began to fall. It was very cold and you could only keep warm by lighting a fire. There was little food to be found and most of that was covered by deep snow.

The grasshopper remembered how hard the ants had worked during the long, hot summer while he had sat under a tree. Suddenly, he had an idea. The ants had collected plenty of food so he would go and visit them.

When the grasshopper reached the ants' nest, he rang the bell. The ants were all cosy and warm inside. One of them opened the door and asked what the grasshopper wanted. The grasshopper replied that he was hungry and wanted to share the ants' food.

All the Chief Ants had a meeting to decide what to do. They remembered the lazy grasshopper as he had watched them working during the summer. He had not done any work at all. So they reluctantly decided that as he had not helped them, nor saved any food for himself, they would not help him now and sent him away to find his own food.

The Eagle and the Fox

A fox had just killed a deer when an eagle, who had been watching from a tree, asked the fox if he would share his prey. The fox agreed, on condition that he could share any food the eagle caught. This was agreed so the deer was carefully divided between the two animals.

The eagle and the fox then decided it would be a good idea to live near each other, especially if they were going to share their food. It would also strengthen their friendship. They found an oak tree in the middle of a deep valley. At the top of the tree, the eagle built a nest and the fox dug a hole near a rock where he hid his young foxes.

The young foxes used to play outside their den and one day, while the fox was out hunting, the eagle, forgetting their agreement, swooped down and carried off the young foxes to his nest where he fed them to his young eagles.

In the meantime, the fox had captured a hare in the woods and was returning to his den to share the food with his friend, the eagle. You can imagine the poor fox's sadness when he discovered his cubs were gone. He soon realised what had happened and was determined to repay the eagle for betraying his trust.

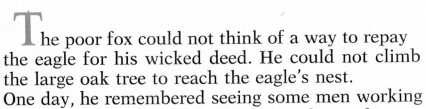

The poor fox could not think of a way to repay the eagle for his wicked deed. He could not climb the large oak tree to reach the eagle's nest.
One day, he remembered seeing some men working in the woods who had built a large fire to burn their rubbish.

He decided to visit this place to see what he could find. He eventually decided to steal a large **branch** which had been in the fire and was still burning. He dragged this back to the valley.

When he finally reached the oak tree, he lay the burning branch in the dry grass which soon caught fire. There was a strong wind which blew the flames towards the oak tree which also caught fire. Soon the eagle returned but was unable to save the baby eagles.

The eagle was very angry and shouted at the fox, accusing him of killing his babies. The fox replied that he had only done the same as the eagle had done in the first place.

Both creatures were sad at losing their babies.

In the book of wise sayings, it is written that anyone who betrays a friendship will receive just punishment.